6/19

D0375819

With special thanks to Michael Ford

For Frank Owen

www.seaquestbooks.co.uk

ORCHARD BOOKS

First published in Great Britain in 2014 by Orchard Books
This edition published in 2017 by The Watts Publishing Group

3 5 7 9 10 8 6 4

Text © 2014 Beast Quest Limited.
Cover and inside illustrations by Artful Doodlers,
with special thanks to Bob and Justin © Orchard Books 2014

Sea Quest is a registered trademark of Beast Quest Limited
Series created by Beast Quest Limited, London

The moral rights of the author and illustrator have been asserted.
All characters and events in this publication, other than those clearly in the public domain,
are fictitious and any resemblance to real persons, living or dead, is purely coincidental.

All rights reserved.
No part of this publication may be reproduced, stored in a retrieval system, or transmitted, in any form
or by any means, without the prior permission in writing of the publisher, nor be otherwise circulated in
any form of binding or cover other than that in which it is published and without a similar condition
including this condition being imposed on the subsequent purchaser.

A CIP catalogue record for this book is available from the British Library.

ISBN 978 1 40832 851 4

Printed in Great Britain by Clays Ltd, St Ives plc

MIX
Paper from
responsible sources
FSC® C104740

The paper and board used in this book are made from wood from responsible sources

Orchard Books
An imprint of Hachette Children's Group
Part of The Watts Publishing Group Limited
Carmelite House, 50 Victoria Embankment, London EC4Y 0DZ

An Hachette UK Company
www.hachette.co.uk
www.hachettechildrens.co.uk

SKALDA
THE SOUL STEALER

NORTHERN PLAINS
PUBLIC LIBRARY
Ault, Colorado

BY ADAM BLADE

ORCHARD

>COMMENCE VIDEO TRANSMISSION

Mistress Cora! Sumara is ours. The Professor's monster lurks beneath the depths. King Salinus is enslaved to its will, along with all his people.

The beast is more terrifying than I could ever have imagined. Even I, Regulis, shudder at the sight of those huge eyes...able to control your very being!

Now we must wait... That Breather boy Max and the princess Lia will come meddling soon enough. Fools! Nothing can prepare them for the nightmare that awaits.

Skalda the Soul Stealer will be their doom!

>END TRANSMISSION

>LOG ENTRY ENDS

STORY 1:

THE BEAST BELOW

CHAPTER ONE

DISTRESS CALL

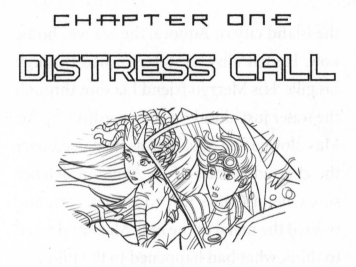

Max sped away from Aquora on his aquabike. Skirting just above the ocean floor, he took in the sights around him. Schools of fish drifted through the deep, an octopus lay almost perfectly camouflaged in the hollow of a boulder, shells large and small were scattered on the seabed, and corals of every colour in the rainbow sprouted like underwater trees. His dogbot Rivet darted like a torpedo between the branches.

Though Max had lived most of his life on

the island city of Aquora, the sea was home now. He felt alive as water rushed through his gills. His Merryn friend Lia shot through the water just ahead on her swordfish, Spike. Max slowed the aquabike as he passed over the charred carcass of an Aquoran defence sub. One of Cora's torpedoes had torn and twisted the metal of the hull. Max shuddered to think what had happened to the pilot.

We won that battle, Max told himself. *But the war isn't over.*

Cora Blackheart, the most fearsome pirate on the ocean planet of Nemos, had tried to destroy Aquora. Many lives had been lost trying to stop her deadly Robobeast Chakrol, a hammerhead shark with robotic weaponry, designed by Max's evil uncle, the Professor.

"Bad lady gone?" barked Rivet.

Max shook his head. They'd caught the

Professor and locked him up in Aquora's jail, but Cora had escaped capture.

"For now, Riv," said Max, "but she'll be back as sure as the tide comes in."

"What's the hold-up?" came Lia's voice.

Max tore his gaze from the remains of the

sub. The Merryn girl was floating up ahead on Spike, her silver hair rippling in the current and a look of frustration on her face. She was clearly eager to get to their destination – her home city of Sumara, kingdom of the Merryn. Max glided over and banked the aquabike next to his friend.

"Are you all right?" he asked.

Lia sighed. "It's just the message I got," she replied. "What does it mean? It's freaking me out."

Max nodded. After the battle with Cora, a pufferfish messenger had come for Lia with a summons from her father, King Salinus. It was brief and confused – something about trouble in Sumara.

"It may be nothing," said Max. "Cora's pirates all ran away and my uncle's locked up."

Lia looked at him with wide, fearful eyes. "My father wouldn't call me back home for *nothing*," she said. "Besides, I just know something's wrong. I can feel it."

Max had learned to trust Lia's mysterious Aqua Powers – the way the Merryn controlled and communicated with the creatures of the sea. Lia was only just learning to use them properly, but her powers had already got her and Max out of several scrapes.

"Let's hurry," said Lia. "The sooner we get there, the sooner I can put my mind at rest." She patted her swordfish's side, and with a flick of his powerful tail, Spike shot off into open water.

Max pressed the bike's throttle to full and the thrusters pushed even faster. Beside them, Rivet tucked his paws up towards his belly for maximum streamlining. They dipped over an ocean shelf and descended into the gloomy depths.

It's a good thing Lia's leading the way, thought

Max. Even though Max had visited Sumara before, it didn't appear on any maps, and he doubted he could have found the hidden city alone.

The animal life got weirder the deeper they went. They passed a pod of albino whales, great pale bullet shapes hanging in the water. Then they saw jellyfish with phosphorescent bodies pulsing gently along.

"Not far now!" Lia called back.

Then she suddenly stopped in a cloud of bubbles, and Max had to yank on the bike's brakes to stop himself crashing into her.

"What did you do that for?" he asked.

Lia cocked her head. "Listen. Can you hear that?"

Not your over-sensitive Aqua Powers again! Max thought.

But then he heard it too – music, not far ahead. An eerie, haunting melody that seemed to fill the water. It was strangely familiar.

"It's beautiful," Max muttered. Barely thinking, he turned the aquabike towards the sound and pressed the throttle. In a second, Lia shot ahead to block his path.

"Don't you recognise it?" she said. "That's Grundle music!"

Max just smiled, still enchanted by the sound. "Oh, yes. I think you're right."

"We need to keep our heads," said Lia. "Grundle music can be dangerous, remember."

Max tried to ignore the music. Lia was right – the Grundle could bewitch listeners and make them lose their senses. And once you were in their clutches, they always made you pay for your release.

"We need to keep going," he said. "Maybe we can find a way around them."

Staying out of sight, Max let the aquabike drift over a rocky outcrop and there they were. A troop of Grundle sat in a circle on a patch of the seabed. Their huge forms and crushing limbs resembled figures carved from rock. Max always thought they looked clumsy, but their music was delicate. Instruments crafted from seashells sat in their laps. Some Grundle beat sharkskin drums, while others plucked at strings woven from seaweed. Beside them, Max noticed several open sacks brimming with shining crystals.

Lia put her finger to her lips, fear in her eyes, and pointed in the other direction. Max got the message: *Avoid them!*

But those crystals... he thought. He felt a flash of recognition, as if he'd seen them before, but he couldn't think where.

His mind was still searching when Rivet

barked. The Grundle all turned as one. The hairs on the back of Max's neck rose up in panic.

"We'd better get out of here," he said. But it was too late. The Grundle snatched up their instruments and, seeing their audience, began to play again. Max felt his strength ebb away. He felt weak and powerless.

Glancing across, he saw that Lia looked even worse; she was barely clinging onto Spike's back. Summoning his strength, Max leaned over and helped Lia onto the back of the aquabike, where she collapsed gratefully.

"It's the music," Lia mumbled.

The Grundle swarmed around them in a tight circle, putting their instruments away. Instead they drew their long coral knives.

"I recognise them," said one, in a voice like gravel. Its eyes burned with anger.

"They're the ones who swim with the thief," said another.

Max struggled to understand what they meant.

"Their pirate friend stole the stinger from us," said the first Grundle.

Uh oh! thought Max, realising what they were talking about. "They mean Roger," he said to Lia. "He stole the tentacle from them, remember – the one that came from Stinger the jellyfish Robobeast."

Lia held out her webbed hands defensively. "Listen to me. Roger is *not* our friend," she told the Grundle.

Max was surprised she spoke so firmly. It was true Roger wasn't the most reliable of companions, but he'd put his life on the line for them more than once. He just happened to be a thief too.

The Grundle looked at each other, then one spoke. "Not your friend, yet you know his name. We think you lie."

"They must pay the debt," said another. "You owe the Grundle."

The large shapes began to close in on all sides. One raised its curved dagger. Rivet growled and pressed closer to Max on the aquabike.

Roger's light fingers might cost us our

lives! thought Max, preparing to draw his hyperblade.

Suddenly the ocean shook. Below them the seabed quaked and split. Bubbles poured out of a yawning canyon, and a moment later Max saw a swirl of water rising from the chasm. *A whirlpool!*

He felt the current tug at the bike, gently at first, then with astonishing power. The Grundle cried out as one, panicking as they tried to swim upwards.

"Lia! Riv! Spike! To me!" Max cried.

The whirlpool gripped them like a fist and yanked them towards the seabed.

CHAPTER TWO

SUMARA ABANDONED

Max revved the bike against the current. Spike closed his teeth over the back of the aquabike, tail thrashing frantically. Rivet switched on the magnets in his paws and clamped down too. Through the spinning mass of sand and rock and weed, Max saw the sucking hole draw closer – a mouth hungry to consume them. "Hold on!" he shouted, but he could barely hear his own voice above the rushing water. He turned the throttle to full power and revved as hard as he could. The bike's nose pushed a fraction at a time towards the edge of the whirlpool. Max leaned over the handlebars, throwing his weight forward, and Lia held on tight. With a jerk, the bike broke free of the water's grip.

The Grundle wailed and groaned. Looking over his shoulder, Max could see they were fighting a losing battle against the suction power of the water. Fear showed on their strange faces as they flailed about, trying to break loose. Two or three were spinning round and round, their bodies a blur and their pitiful cries distorted.

Max eased up on the throttle and let the aquabike sink back towards the ocean floor, his eyes locked on the spiralling Grundle.

"What are you doing?" Lia shouted.

"I'm not sure," said Max, "but I can't just

leave them there!"

The first of the Grundle was nearing the hole, being dragged along the seabed. The swirling water was yanking down boulders and tearing the ground apart. His bike was too heavy to manoeuvre in the current – he needed something smaller and lighter.

"Riv! Go and fetch the Grundle!" said Max.

Rivet disengaged his magnets and dived, snout-first. Through the spinning debris, Max saw him grip one of the Grundle by its clothes and yank it away from the chasm. But there were still half a dozen Grundle losing their fight against the ferocity of the water. Max was holding the bike steady when a plan came to him. He pulled the lever on the console to release the bike's towing chain. It snaked out into the water, tugged down by the whirlpool.

"All of you!" he shouted at the top of his

voice. "Get a grip and hang on!"

The Grundle looked up and saw the chain.
One by one they managed to throw out arms
and grip it. One was in a helpless spin, but
another managed to grab its leg. As each new
Grundle joined, Max felt the bike tug harder,
pulled back towards the swirling mass.

"Max, do something!" cried Lia. "We're

going to get dragged in too!"

"No we won't," Max yelled back, trying to sound more confident than he felt. He gunned the thrusters as far as they'd go as the last Grundle clasped the chain. The bike's engine whined, but they didn't move.

We need more power!

The bike juddered and fell back a little, closer to the hole. The Grundle all wailed as one and Max's heart leaped in fear.

He reached into the bike's compartment, and took out a marine grenade.

"What are you going to do?" shouted Lia in alarm. "Blow us up?"

"No," said Max. "I'm going to blow us *sideways*."

He pulled the pin and hurled the grenade to one side and up as hard as he could.

Five… he counted.

Max watched the grenade drift away.

Four…

Still not a safe distance!

Three…

The bike's engine juddered. It couldn't keep going at this power.

Two…

The grenade floated ten bike-lengths away.

One…

BOOM!

The water exploded white and Max felt the force of the blast hit him like a wave. It threw them sideways, and suddenly they were free of the whirlpool's grip. Max and Lia were hurled from the bike's seats and rolled over and over in the foaming water.

When Max righted himself, he saw the Grundle sagging on the seabed, exhausted. The whirlpool still raged not far off, but they were well clear of its sucking power.

The Grundle who Rivet had rescued swam

towards Max. *Surely he can't still want to fight,* thought Max. He cast a glance at his aquabike, which rested on its side. *If I could get to my hyperblade…*

But the Grundle seemed to have changed his tune, shaken by the whirlpool. "We misjudged you both," he said. "You have shown by your actions that you are noble creatures, unlike your pirate friend."

Max breathed a sigh of relief.

"He's not our friend," Lia said again.

The Grundle held up his large hand. "No matter, Merryn child," he said. "You saved our lives and now it is we who are in your debt. We offer you this gift as payment."

The Grundle drew out a small box carved from a gleaming shell. "This is a singing box of the Grundle," he said. "Open it anywhere in the oceans of Nemos and the Grundle will come to your aid."

Max took the box. It weighed next to nothing. "Thank you," he said.

He felt a tug at his sleeve. Lia was frowning. "We need to get on our way to Sumara," she said.

Max nodded. He smiled at the Grundle, who was already drifting back to his fellows. "Goodbye!" he called.

"Farewell," replied the Grundle as one.

Max straightened the aquabike and stowed the music box away. "Let's go!" he said.

Soon they were shooting downwards again, with Lia leading the way in silence.

Max guessed she was too worried to talk.

It wasn't long before the gleaming coral towers of Sumara rose high in the water ahead. At first he was relieved, but Max's relief soon turned to something darker.

Something's wrong, he realised at once.

One of the main palace towers was gone. Max's blood thumped through his veins as they descended. The base of the tower remained but the rest lay in ruins where it had collapsed. The main streets, normally thronging with Merryn, were empty. The sea flowers which lined the avenues had been torn up in places, almost as if the city had been attacked. Sumara was silent – no conversation, no music, no laughter. The only sound was the hum of the aquabike's engines. Max bristled, and reached for his hyperblade. Despite the silence, he felt they were being watched.

"I told you something was wrong," said Lia. There were tears in her eyes.

"What happened here?" Max asked. "Another Robobeast?"

They passed beneath the looming Arch of Peace, which had a crack across its centre.

Seaweed flags lay strewn on the seabed. Max felt a chill settle over his skin. Surely Cora hadn't had time to mount another attack?

Unless it was planned all along, he thought. *It would be just like Cora to be one step ahead.*

"We have to find my father," said Lia.

They were headed toward the palace when another rumble shook the water around them. Max's heart jumped.

"What's going on?" he said. "That sounded just like the explosion that started the whirlpool."

Lia shook her head. "I don't know, but I don't like it. Something bad is going on here."

They reached the palace, which was eerily silent. Leaving Spike and Rivet at the doorway, Lia and Max climbed the wide staircase towards the throne chamber. Normally, guards with pearl lances would have lined the steps, but today there were none. More cracks snaked across the walls, as if a powerful earthquake had struck Sumara.

It's like a ghost town, thought Max. *Sumara's been abandoned.*

But when they reached the chamber, Lia gasped and Max saw that he was wrong.

On the throne sat a Merryn he didn't recognise. He was tall, younger than King Salinus, with lithe, powerful limbs. His robes were a sparkling golden colour. But his small, squinting eyes and thin lips, curled into a sneer, made him look far from friendly. Around his neck hung a chain of glittering crystal.

It's the same crystal the Grundle were guarding, Max realised.

A dozen or so other Merryn stood around the stranger, still and silent.

"Regulis!" said Lia. "How dare you sit in my father's throne!"

The Merryn stood up slowly and pasted on a charming smile.

"Daughter of Salinus," he said. "What a pleasant surprise. I'm afraid your father is unwell. In his absence, the council have asked me to take charge."

The other Merryn all nodded as one.

"But you have no royal blood!" said Lia. "It's not right!"

Max saw her face was flushed with anger and put a restraining hand on her arm. "Let's hear him out," he said quietly. "Maybe your father sent you the message because he was ill."

"A message?" said Regulis, his smile disappearing for a split second, then quickly returning. "You must be hungry and tired from your journey. Please, we're about to eat in the banqueting hall. Join us."

"I want to see my father," said Lia coldly.

Regulis's smile remained. "Your father has seen Tarla the healer," he said. "For now, he's sleeping. After you eat, I'm sure he'll be well enough for visitors."

Max could see Lia was about to say something more, but then she nodded. "Very well."

Regulis led them through to a large chamber in which was a huge table loaded with platters of seaweed cakes. Max groaned inwardly. He'd become used to it, but he'd never *like* Merryn cuisine. Seaweed cakes tasted like cardboard with mulched-up grass on top. They looked particularly unpleasant after his brief reunion with rich Aquoran food. Regulis summoned a servant and muttered in his ear. Two more places were quickly laid at the table. Max and Lia took their seats.

I am quite hungry, thought Max. *I suppose*

even a seaweed cake will do.

The Merryn courtiers tucked into their cakes, and Lia and Max did the same.

At his first bite, the cake tasted even more bitter than normal, but Max forced himself to chew and swallow. Lia didn't seem bothered. She was chewing her cake while keeping a hostile glare on Regulis. *It is strange that he was sitting on the throne like that*, thought Max.

He looked at Regulis himself and saw that the councillor was watching them intently, the same smile on his lips. The same *cruel* smile.

Something isn't right here, Max thought, *and I don't need any Aqua Powers to tell me that.*

A sudden bang on the table jolted him to alertness. He turned to see that Lia had fallen face-first onto her plate.

"Lia?" said Max. His voice sounded distant to his own ears. A sudden thought hit him as another mouthful of seaweed cake slid down his throat. It didn't just taste bad. It tasted *wrong*.

Poisoned!

His vision blurred. Max could just make out the grinning image of Regulis.

Max dropped the remains of his seaweed cake, feeling dizzy.

"What have you done to us?" he slurred.

"Nothing to worry about," said Regulis. "Time to sleep now."

Max clambered to his feet and tried to leap at the councillor. He staggered a couple of steps, then the floor rose to meet him, and blackness clouded his vision.

CHAPTER THREE

DEATH SENTENCE

Max could hear Lia groaning. Someone was shaking him.

Where am I?

As his vision swam into focus, Max made out bars. Metal bars. *A prison cell?*

A Merryn guard stood over him. Lia sat at his side. Together they were hoisted to their feet and pushed out of the cell. Max felt for his hyperblade, but it was gone. He realised where they were – the same prison he had been held in the first time he came to Sumara.

But why am I in here again?

"You can't do this!" said Lia, struggling to pull herself free. "I'm a princess of Sumara! My father is the King."

The guards ignored her, as if they couldn't even hear. They just stared straight ahead. Max tried to struggle away too, but the guard's grip was titanium-strong. Max wondered where Rivet and Spike had got to. *Hopefully they escaped!*

They were marched out of the prison and along a rocky corridor, before emerging at a side gate to the palace. The guards escorted them along Treaty Avenue, still deserted, towards Thallos Square. The statue of the Merryn god Thallos – with his sleek, dolphin body and strange beaked head – stood on his pedestal surrounded by hundreds of Merryn.

So that's where everyone is!

Most of Sumara's citizens were here, Max guessed. Oddly, they didn't make a sound, not even muttering to one another. They just stared glassily at Max and Lia.

Max saw Tarla, the healing woman, standing near the front. "Hey!" he said. "Help us, please! Tell them who we are."

Tarla's features didn't even twitch in recognition.

"What's wrong with you all?" shouted Lia.

The guards pushed them up against the statue of Thallos and quickly tied them there with strands of knotted, leathery seaweed. Max strained against his bonds, but the seaweed must have been a special variety. It was as strong as mooring chains. Strands across his chest and more around his waist and legs kept him pinned firmly in place.

A horn sounded. Not the normal sweet music of Sumara, but a harsh blare like a

ship's foghorn. The main doors of the palace opened and out stepped Regulis with the other councillors behind him. Last of all came King Salinus, head held high. He didn't look ill at all.

"Father!" Lia called. "At last! Tell them to let us go!"

King Salinus turned a cold gaze upon them, but didn't utter a word.

"Dad?" said Lia, her lips trembling. "What's

wrong with you?"

"He's brainwashed or something," said Max, horror tightening his chest as he realised what was wrong with the Merryn. "They all are."

He managed to move his hand a little. Not enough to free himself, but enough to press the communicator on his wrist. "Riv, come in!" he whispered, hoping his dogbot was listening. "Get to Thallos Square as soon as you can. And bring me a weapon!"

Regulis approached them, eyes alive with cruelty. A terrible thought occurred to Max. What if they'd captured Rivet too?

"People of Sumara!" Regulis said. "As you know, our enemies are everywhere. Even among us. These two *traitors* might have gills, but they have the souls of Breathers. They are our deadliest foes. And what do we do to our foes?"

"Kill them!" droned the Merryn crowd. "Kill them! Kill them!"

To his horror, Max saw that King Salinus was joining in the chant, calling for his daughter's death. *This is some sort of nightmare...*

"We're not your enemies!" said Lia desperately. "We're friends of Sumara. We saved you all in the past."

Regulis reached into his tunic. "The past

doesn't matter now," he said. "The future is what's important." He drew out a long, ivory-handled coral sword that gleamed wickedly. "And I'm afraid your futures are going to be rather short."

Lia thrashed and heaved, but the seaweed cords held her tightly. Max tried to jerk free too, but the bonds bit into his wrists and made him wince in pain. "The Merryn don't kill people," said Lia. "My father is King and he's never put anyone to death."

"He's not King any more," said Regulis. "I'm the ruler of Sumara now. Don't worry." He reached out with the dagger blade towards her throat. "This will be quick."

Max swallowed, eyes on the dagger. *It can't end like this!*

The heads of the gathered Merryn jerked to one side in unison as a metal shape ploughed into Regulis's side, sending the

sword spinning out of his grasp and toppling the councillor. Regulis snarled in fury.

"Rivet here! Rivet rescue!" barked the dogbot.

"Just in time!" said Max. "Get us out of here!"

As Rivet tore at Max's bonds with his metal jaws, a silvery shape flashed around the statue of Thallos. *Spike!* The swordfish made short work of Lia's seaweed chains.

Regulis, shaking his head clear, crawled across the ground and retrieved his sword. He spun the blade in his palm. "Maybe your death won't be so quick, after all," he said.

He stalked closer, and the other Merryn pressed in on all sides, blocking any escape route.

Rivet swam beside Max, and his back compartment slid open.

"Brought sword, Max!"

Max smiled grimly, reaching inside and taking out his hyperblade. "Good work, Riv," he said, and turned to face Regulis. "If you want a fight, come and get me!"

CHAPTER FOUR

ON THE RUN

Regulis leaped forward, swinging his long coral sword.

Max blocked it with the hyperblade, but the blow knocked him off his feet and tumbling into the statue of Thallos. Regulis was strong!

Lia was watching, looking worried, but if she tried to help, the Merryn guards would grab her – Spike and Rivet too.

"I'm going to enjoy killing you!" said Regulis. "I never liked Breathers!"

As the Merryn aimed a vertical swipe at Max's head, he rolled sideways and regained his feet. The coral blade bit deep into Thallos's tail with a dull *clang*.

That could have been my skull, thought Max.

Regulis managed to free the blade and came at Max with a long sweeping attack.

Max ducked and weaved to avoid it, parrying with his hyperblade. Regulis kept coming. Each block sent a shockwave down Max's arm. The coral blade was longer, so it was almost impossible to get close. But it looked heavier too. With one attack, Regulis over-reached and lost his balance. Max darted in and nicked the Merryn's arm with the tip of his blade.

Regulis winced and gnashed his teeth. "I'll slice you up, Breather!"

The rest of the Merryn enclosed them, looking on vacantly.

It's like they don't care who wins, thought Max, as he leaped back to avoid another slash.

Regulis was red-faced from either humiliation or exhaustion.

"Citizens of Sumara!" he shouted. "Help me finish him!"

The crowd, who until a moment ago could have been fast asleep, suddenly stepped forward as one, closing the ring more tightly around Max and Regulis. Then they stepped forward again.

There are too many of them! thought Max.

"Riv, help!" said Max, turning on the spot as the Merryn horde swooped in, webbed hands clawing at him. His dogbot shot over the heads of the crowd, tail wagging. Max pushed off the seabed and grabbed Rivet's collar, tucking his hyperblade in his belt. He felt hands clutching at his ankles, but the dogbot propelled himself away and pulled Max free.

Rivet carried Max high over the statue of Thallos. Max was glad when he saw Lia shooting clear of the crowd as well, riding on Spike. He looked back and saw the Merryn watching them with empty expressions.

"Get them!" yelled Regulis from below. "Dead or alive!"

The Merryn surged from the square like a flock of birds taking off. They darted as one towards Max and Lia, closing by the second.

"I can't leave my father!" said Lia, pointing to where King Salinus was standing at the edge of the crowd.

"Can't you see?" said Max desperately.

"He's one of them now. We need to regroup somewhere safe and make a plan. But first we've got to find my aquabike!"

The words had barely left his mouth when Rivet yanked him away again, zipping through the water at maximum speed and leaving the pursuing Merryn horde behind. Lia waited a moment longer, her eyes lingering on her father.

"Come on!" said Max.

Just before the mob caught her, Lia sped after him on Spike.

The Merryn gave chase.

"Riv, lose them!" said Max.

Rivet dipped close towards the seabed, weaving around rocks and plunging through seaweed. He flipped and shot sideways, far into the distance. Spike cut through the water in their wake.

Rivet zigzagged over a boulder field, tail

propeller churning up bubbles behind. Max checked over his shoulder and found that the Merryn were nowhere to be seen.

"You did it, Riv!" he said.

But the dogbot didn't slow. He climbed a low rise at speed and then shot down the other side. Only after another few twists and turns did he drift to a halt. Spike hovered beside them, eyes bright and alive with the chase.

Max realised where they were.

The Graveyard!

The Merryn had given that name to the dumping ground where they threw all the unwanted and unusable tech that came their way, scavenged from the oceans. Max saw plenty of cabling and pieces of old ships scattered about. There were parts of engines, some blackened by fire; watertight barrels and antennae; loading platforms and ladders and broken plexiglass. There were weapons too, if you looked close enough. Ancient torpedo chutes, trigger mechanisms and blasters. Max could have spent all day hunting through the wreckage in search of spare parts for his inventions.

"Why have you brought us here, Rivet?" said Lia.

Rivet broke away from them and swam down into the garbage pit. "Max bike!" he barked.

Then Max saw it too, half submerged under old sheets of scarred metal. "The aquabike!" he said, swimming down too. "Riv must have sniffed it out. Lia, help me dig it free."

Together they tossed the sheet metal aside and pulled the bike clear. "The Merryn must have dumped it here," Max said. He got on, checking the diagnostics. "It still works fine."

But Lia was swimming off in the other

direction. "Hang on!" she called back. "What's this?"

Max gunned the bike closer, and saw her hovering over what looked like a communication screen which had been buried in the rubble and debris. Unlike most of the broken old junk in the Graveyard, it looked brand new – pristine, even.

"Switch it on," said Max.

"How?" asked Lia.

Max rolled his eyes. "With the...er... switch."

Lia pressed the button at the side of the screen and with a few green flashes it came to life. A face appeared, one they knew all too well. Max could barely believe what he was seeing. The face had dark eyes and was surrounded by tumbling hair like a black waterfall.

Cora Blackheart.

Max felt his fists clench.

"Greetings, Regulis," Cora said, sounding bored. "You're not due to report for another two days. I hope nothing is..." She paused, her eyes widening. "You two!"

"What are you up to, Cora?" asked Max. He grabbed both sides of the screen, bringing his face close.

Cora's mouth split into a smile, revealing her ruby jewel tooth. "A plan that you can't foil," she said. "You might have defeated my scheme to use the Kraken's Eye, but this time you've swum right into my net! Something lurks under Sumara, and soon you'll meet it."

The screen went blank.

"She's in league with Regulis!" said Lia. She flicked her feet to swim up above the Graveyard, glancing around nervously. "I never liked him!"

"But what did she mean about something lurking under Sumara?" said Max. He tried switching the screen off and on again, but it seemed dead.

Rivet let out a low warning growl.

"Oh no!" said Lia, pointing. "They've found us!"

Max swam up to her, and saw a swarm of angry Merryn approaching, all clutching pearl spears.

He turned and his heart skipped a beat. More Merryn were swimming from the other direction. Regulis had them surrounded.

Max grabbed Lia and pulled her back

down towards the seabed, among the mounds of discarded tech. "We've got to get out of here," he said. "Otherwise this will be our graveyard too."

CHAPTER FIVE

INTO THE BEAST'S LAIR

Max scrambled over the discarded rubbish, his heart hammering as he looked for a hiding place. Lia did the same, while Rivet and Spike nosed bits of scrap metal aside.

"I've found something!" Lia called.

"Leave it!" said Max. "We need somewhere to hide."

But Lia stretched out her hand, palm down. "Can't you feel that? A draught!"

Frantic, Max kicked towards her. He held out his own hand and felt it too – a cold current coming from the seabed.

"Help me!" he said, crouching on the ground and tugging the screen aside. The current grew stronger, and beneath the screen he saw a black hole, tunnelling into the ocean floor. He couldn't tell how big it

was, because more debris covered most of the opening. He felt a chill of fear as he stared into the darkness.

"Where does it go?" whispered Lia.

"I've no idea," said Max, "but look at the sides." The torn-up ground was solid rock, scarred as if by many small drills. "This isn't natural," he said. "Someone made this."

"Or some*thing*," said Lia, swallowing. "I don't like it. We've no idea what's down there."

"There they are!" said a voice from above. It was a band of Merryn soldiers, each riding a swordfish and clutching a pearl lance, racing over from the edge of the Graveyard.

"The elite guard!" said Lia.

Desperation clawed at Max's stomach. He peered into the black hole in the ocean floor, then shared a glance with Lia. "We don't have a choice," he said. "Get in!"

Lia dropped into the tunnel foot-fins first, followed by Spike. Rivet barked as Max quickly leaped back onto the aquabike and aimed it towards the approaching Merryn. They were now only a short distance away. *This should scare them off.* He fired the blasters across their path. The shots scorched through the water just ahead of them, but they didn't even pause. Max fired again, as close as he dared. He didn't want to risk

accidentally hitting one of them. Still the Merryn swam on towards him, undaunted. They were only a few strokes away…

So much for slowing them down.

He steered the bike towards the tunnel, but a pearl spear thudded into the left stabiliser, thrown by the closest Merryn. Several warning lights flashed as the bike veered sideways, launching him off the seat. The bike nosed down into the Graveyard with a

crunch. Max didn't want to leave it, but there was no time. If he tried to get it back now, he'd end up with a Merryn spear through his chest.

He clambered into the hole after Lia and Spike. He saw Rivet trying to drag a one-man sub towards the tunnel entrance with his teeth. The Merryn were drawing back their arms, ready to throw their spears.

"Leave it, Riv!" said Max. "There isn't time."

Whining in frustration, Rivet let go and swam after Max, just as the Merryn closed in. Two spears barely missed him as he zoomed into the hole. Looking back, he saw that the Merryn had stopped and were peering down after them into the chasm. For the first time, they looked unsure of themselves – afraid, even.

Perhaps they know what's down here, thought Max grimly.

Rolling over in the water, he swam after Lia into the darkness.

"Riv, give us some light," he whispered.

A second later, Rivet's snout illuminated the way ahead, picking out Spike's silvery shape and Lia clutching his tail.

The tunnel drilled straight down, before

levelling out and widening. The walls were scarred, but when he peered closer, Max didn't see how any tool could have made such marks. They were irregular, as if metal claws had gouged out the rock.

"We may as well keep going," said Lia, but Max detected the quaver in her voice. *She's scared*, he thought. *And I know exactly how she feels.*

They swam more slowly, with Rivet's lamp sweeping arcs through the gloomy, lifeless waters.

"It feels like we must be right beneath Sumara," said Lia. Her voice sounded oddly hollow in the emptiness.

"I was thinking the same," said Max. "Did you know this was here?"

Lia shook her head. "We must be almost as deep as the crystal forests," she said. The tunnel sides suddenly fell away and they found themselves swimming into an enormous cavern. Max could dimly see the far side and the roof high above. Distant rumbles echoed through the water.

"More earthquakes," Max mumbled. *But what's causing them?*

He sensed movement below and glanced down. He was sure he saw something – a couple of spiky objects – crossing the cavern. But then they were gone. His pulse started to race.

"Riv," he called. "Shine a light down there, will you?"

Rivet's lamp shone an arc through the dark water. He pointed it downwards, illuminating the cavern floor deep below them. At first all Max could see was a landscape of brown rocks, covered in a thin layer of moss. Then the light stopped and Lia gasped.

Max's heart thumped in his chest and his

body jerked back in shock. He was looking at
an enormous green light, a huge black oval
at its centre.

Fear coursed through Max's veins when he realised what he was looking at.

A gigantic green eye.

CHAPTER SIX

MIND CONTROL

"Don't move!" hissed Max.

Maybe it hasn't seen us...

The eye stared straight ahead, vacant, but suddenly a colossal shape lurched forward. Rivet tried to track it with his snout-lamp but it moved too fast. Max saw flashes of an enormous body passing beneath them.

"What *is* that thing?" whispered Lia.

Then the lamp caught the telltale gleam of silver metal covering parts of the creature. The browns and greens of the moss-covered rocks were reflected in the shiny surfaces.

Max's heart thudded in his throat. "It's a Robobeast," he said.

The Professor's work.

The thing moved again – it looked like the rock rippling. They were stuck in here with this terrible creation, and there was no escape.

We need to get away!

Max swam towards Lia, grabbed her hand and pulled her to the edge of the cavern. Rivet followed. Max twisted a knob behind the dogbot's ear, widening the lamp's rays and pointing it below them. The beam picked out the creature in its entirety, and Max stifled a gasp of horror.

It was some sort of giant barracuda fish, its sleek flanks striped with scales. Interlocking titanium plates coated its face and head like a helmet and mask, leaving only its green eyes

and a mouth full of spiked teeth bare. Odd
though – there were wires trailing across the
plates, almost as if the tech work wasn't quite
finished. From between its jaws, Max made
out a green glow in the depths of its mouth.
Etched into the titanium plate that covered

its cheek was the name 'SKALDA'.

Max found himself feeling sorry for the barracuda, trapped inside a metal skull. But this was no time for pity. Max drew his hyperblade, before moving forward to get a better look.

He swam a fraction closer.

"What are you *doing*?" said Lia.

"I'm not entirely sure," said Max, "but the Professor's work isn't normally so shoddy. I think he maybe got called away before he'd had chance to complete the robotics. Can you use your Aqua Powers to talk to it?"

Lia frowned. "I could try."

With gentle strokes they swam together towards the Robobeast. Skalda hardly moved – its body was the size of a transport sub, dwarfing Max as he approached.

It looks scared, Max thought. *The sooner we put its mind at ease, the better.*

Lia floated in front of the Robobeast, and stared into the eyes behind the mask.

It's big enough to swallow her in a single mouthful...

Max thought he heard a click, then a low mechanical hum. *It must be some sort of malfunction.*

"Tell it we'll try to take off the robotics," said Max.

Lia suddenly jerked back, almost as if she'd received an electric shock.

"Are you OK?" he asked her. "What happened?"

Lia turned to him and smiled. "I'm perfectly fine."

"Are you sure?" Max asked, puzzled by her odd smile.

"Quite sure," she said.

Suddenly, she lunged at him. Max felt her hands slip around his throat in a vice-like grip, and she pushed him down towards the bottom of the cavern.

Max tried to prise Lia's fingers away, but she held him firm. "What…are…you…doing?" he gasped, his voice choked. She didn't answer. Max stared at her, looking for some clue, as he felt the blood collect behind his

eyes. Lia's face was completely calm, with no anger or even any hint that she cared about what she was doing. Black spots started to flash across Max's vision as his brain was deprived of oxygen. If he didn't find a way to free himself soon, he'd die down here in the dark cavern. He was vaguely aware of Rivet barking madly nearby, obviously unsure what to do.

She's not going to stop, he realised. *She's trying to kill me. I've got to fight back.*

Max drew back his leg and kicked out, catching Lia's stomach with the heel of his foot. The grip on his throat loosened as she tumbled back in the water.

"What…what are you doing?" he croaked, massaging his neck where her fingers had been.

Lia remained a short distance away, not speaking. Her eyes were unfocused, directed not *at* him, but somehow *through* him. It was the same look as on the faces of the bewitched Merryn in Sumara. He sensed a movement below and looked down to see Skalda staring at him as well. Those enormous green eyes seemed wider than before, drilling into his. And now he looked closer, he thought he could see the shadow of intricate wiring, right in the depths of the black pupil. His mind clouded, and he shook his head to clear it.

It's the tech, he realised. *It's somehow twisting my thoughts.*

Max felt a shudder as understanding dawned. *Skalda can control minds!*

He felt his brain grow foggy.

What am I doing here?

His eyes settled on Lia and a fierce determination flooded his heart.

Oh yes, I remember…

He drew his hyperblade and held it aloft,
taking in the look of fear on her face.

I was just about to kill this Merryn girl...

TRAPPED

Max's hatred swelled as he lunged at the Merryn girl. She backed away with a swish of her webbed feet, but came up against the cavern wall.

"Nowhere to run, fish-girl," said Max.

He drew back his arm, ready to stab her.

SLAM!

Max rolled over in the water as something hit him from the side. As he righted himself he saw it was a metal dog with red eyes.

"Max not hurt Lia!" it barked. "Lia friend!"

Max frowned. The dog's name was Rivet – he remembered now. He shook his head, and gradually he began to feel like himself again. Lia was looking at him, eyes round with fear.

What did I just do? Max asked himself, staring at the glowing hyperblade. *I tried to kill my closest friend!*

He thrust the weapon through his belt and swam toward Lia. She looked almost as groggy and confused as he felt.

"Did I just try to strangle you?" she said. "I don't know what came over me."

Max did. He *had* seen wiring in Skalda's eyes, he was sure. He pointed to the barracuda, lurking below them. "I think I understand why it doesn't have any weaponry. Skalda uses its eyes to control minds. We both turned on each other after looking into them. It must be something to do with that weird mask."

A shockwave rippled through the water

from beneath them and when Max looked again, Skalda was gone. *Fast.*

"Uh-oh," said Lia. "I don't like this."

Rivet barked, and directed his snout-lamp sideways. Sure enough, it picked out the Robobeast, stalking silently towards them through the dark water. Spike swam out bravely to position himself in the barracuda's path.

"Don't look into its eyes," said Max.

Skalda twisted in the water and arched its back. Like a fly-swat its tail smacked into Spike and sent him tumbling through the water.

"Spike!" cried Lia, and swam towards her faithful friend, who was plummeting towards the cavern floor.

Then Skalda's face began to change.

The metal plates shifted apart and Max saw a green glow from the depths of the

Robobeast's throat. *What's in there?* he wondered. Suddenly, four robotic tentacles telescoped from inside the barracuda's jaws. Two were tipped with hyperblades, and two with metal pincer claws.

Looks like it's going to kill us the old-fashioned way.

He drew his hyperblade again, ready to defend himself, but Skalda turned and headed for Lia and Spike. Max kicked towards the barracuda in pursuit. One of the tentacles lashed out behind it, towards Max's neck. Caught off guard, he raised his blade just in time to keep his head and felt the beast's hyperblade thump into his own. His shoulder was almost wrenched out of place.

Another tentacle snaked around Max's waist and yanked him through the water. He saw the cavern wall approaching, fast enough to smash his brains out, and he jammed the

tip of his hyperblade into the tentacle's metal
joints. It loosened just enough to allow him
to pull himself free. Desperately he tried to
slow himself, raising his legs and kicking off
the cavern wall. He ducked to avoid another
swipe, and swam like crazy towards Lia and
Spike. She was leaning over the swordfish,
stroking his head. Spike still looked dazed
from being swatted.

"Lia, look out!" Max cried. "Skalda's
coming for you."

The Robobeast paused a sub's length away from them, as if it was unsure. Its tentacles sank by its sides, like it was powering down. Lia kept her eyes averted.

Maybe it's run out of batteries, Max thought hopefully.

Suddenly Spike shook himself to life, quivering from nose to tail. Max's heart leaped to see the swordfish was all right. But Spike turned on Lia with a swipe of his sword. She jerked back to avoid being cut by the deadly point..

"Careful, Spike!" she said. "You almost…"

Spike lunged at her, stabbing frantically. Max saw Lia hiss in pain as the sword gashed her arm.

Skalda's controlling him! Max realised. He threw himself at Spike, gripping the swordfish's dorsal fin and pulling him away from Lia. Spike thrashed and tried to twist and slash at Max, but Max wrapped his arms tightly around Spike's middle and wrestled him against the bottom of the cavern.

By the time Max was starting to tire, Spike had stopped struggling and hung limp in Max's grip.

"It looks like the mind control has vanished," Max called up to Lia. "Maybe it's because the robotics weren't completed."

"Let's get out of here while our minds are still our own," said Lia.

As they turned to swim back towards the tunnels, Skalda closed off their path. *He's not going to let us go easily*, Max thought. He tried not to look directly into its huge green eyes. That was quite easy, because all his attention was on the frightening metal tentacles uncoiling once more from behind the Robobeast's head armour. They snaked slowly towards Max and Lia.

"Now what?" Lia said.

Max sensed Rivet's presence at his side, and it gave him an idea. Rivet was the only one of them Skalda hadn't controlled. Maybe there was a good reason for that...

"We'll use Riv," Max said. "He hasn't got a mind to control."

The dogbot looked at him and cocked his head. "Rivet not stupid, Max. Rivet clever dog."

Max rested a hand on his metal snout. "I know you are, Riv. And that's why you're our only hope. I need you to distract Skalda. Okay?"

Rivet's eyes flashed and, with his tail propeller whirring, he shot towards the Robobeast.

Two tentacles whipped around to meet him, and Rivet expertly rolled in the water, under one and over the other. Skalda turned to look for him, just as Max had planned.

"Quick, we need an escape route," he said. "Somewhere my uncle's creation can't follow us."

Lia had already turned to scan the bottom of the cavern with Spike at her side.

Max heard Rivet's panicked whine and saw that one of the tentacles was clutching his back leg. Another was snaking towards him. Max swam towards him and lunged with his hyperblade, knocking the tentacle aside. Rivet managed to wriggle free. All around the water churned as Skalda angrily flailed and thrashed.

"Down here!" Lia called from the bottom of the cavern. "I've found somewhere to hide."

"To Lia, Riv!" said Max.

The dogbot dived and zoomed past a reaching tentacle. Max grabbed his collar as he passed and they descended quickly to Lia's side. She and Spike were squeezing through a narrow gap in the rock.

Max let go of the collar and paused to let Rivet swim through first. As he turned to check where Skalda was, he got a nasty shock. The Robobeast was staring right at him.

Not again, thought Max, unable to tear his gaze from Skalda's. Then his mind went blank.

Perhaps I'll just stay here for a while...

The barracuda's jaws opened, and the spiked teeth glistened as they edged closer.

Nothing to be afraid of, Max thought. *Just a big fish...*

Something fastened around his ankle. At the same moment as the teeth snapped shut, Max felt himself yanked downwards. He saw blood clouding the water and wondered who it belonged to. Suddenly he found himself in a smaller cave, with rough rocky walls coated in seaweeds and mosses. Across the floor was a sparkling dust. Max struggled to make sense of anything.

Lia slapped him around the face. "Max!" she said. "Snap out of it."

Max's head felt stuffed with cotton wool. "What happened?" he mumbled.

Lia was glancing up and down at him,

looking worried. "Skalda almost had your arm," she said.

Max looked at his arm and saw a deep gash in his skin. *Skalda's tooth mark.* As his head cleared, pain lanced through his body. "Aargh!" he cried, feeling faint.

"We need to bandage you up," said Lia.

"There's a medikit…in the aquabike," said Max. He just wanted to lie down. His brain still wasn't working properly, and his body was in shock from the wound.

The small cave shook as Skalda threw itself against the opening. A small shower of rock and dust drifted through the water.

Lia slapped his face again. "Don't go to sleep," she said. " You've lost blood and you're still suffering the after-effects of Skalda's trance."

"A trance?" Max mumbled.

"Just like the rest of Sumara," said Lia, her

eyes wide with fear. "Don't you see? Somehow all the Merryn apart from Regulis are being controlled by this Robobeast. It's obvious!"

Skalda's teeth appeared at the opening, tearing at the rock. A larger piece broke away, widening the gap.

"Obvious?" said Max. His voice seemed low and distant. "What's obvious?"

Lia dragged him deeper into the cave and slapped him again. "I need you, Max," she said. "We've got to get out of here before it's too late!"

As she spoke, one of Skalda's tentacles slipped into the cave, searching for them like a hungry tongue.

STORY 2:

BATTLE FOR SUMARA

CHAPTER ONE

THE POWER OF SONG

Adrenaline started Max to his senses. He pressed himself against the wall of the cave as the robotic arm snaked towards him. The hyperblade on its tip glinted, swishing from side to side. Lia ducked and swam to the far side.

We can't hide forever, thought Max.

The blade edged closer, stabbing at the ground by his feet. Max noticed the sparkling fragments again. *More crystals*, he realised.

The hyperblade brushed his foot and he kicked it away. Like a flash, the tentacle jerked back, aimed at him. "Move, move!" cried Lia urgently.

Max felt glued to the spot, but Rivet shot up and fastened his metal jaws around the tentacle's hyperblade, breaking it off. The robotic arm retreated through the opening.

"Good boy, Rivet," said Lia. She reached for the wall of the cavern and tore out several long strands of seaweed. "Hold still," she said to Max. The blood had stopped pouring from the wound on his arm, but it still throbbed. As she tied the seaweed bandage over the gash, Max gritted his teeth.

"Don't be such a Breather!" Lia said. But with the mixture of the pain and the weird fog left from Skalda's mind control, Max could barely stay upright. He sagged.

"Stay with me, Max," said Lia. "You've lost a lot of blood. Don't go to sleep."

Max's eyelids felt heavy.

"Max!" said Lia. "Listen to my voice."

"Trying…" mumbled Max.

Lia was winding another layer of bandage around his arm. "Focus, Max!" she said, then began to sing loudly:

"In olden times, there dwelt a maid,
Who longed to leave the land,
To swim away and find a life
Of happiness in the sea."

Max had never heard Lia sing before, and the sound was strangely soothing, the notes floating around him like whale-song. It reminded him of his mother singing lullabies to him as a small child. A feeling of safety and warmth settled over him, and for a moment he even forgot about the pain in his arm. Lia carried on.

> *"She dived beneath the waves one day*
> *And joined a Merryn band.*
> *The Merryn king took her as a wife*
> *And she became his queen."*

As the notes hung in the water, Max realised his senses had completely returned. *Weird!* he thought. *It's as if her singing washed away the mind control.*

Skalda's teeth tore at the opening again, and the green eye flashed past, angry and challenging.

"Keep singing," Max said.

Lia looked at him, frowning. "Why?"

"Because I've got a theory." He swam towards the opening.

"Max not go!" barked Rivet.

"I agree," said Lia, gripping Max's ankle. "Are you mad?"

"Just sing," said Max, pulling his leg free. "As loud as you can."

Max's pulse was racing as he reached the entrance. *Get this wrong and I'm dead*, he thought. Skalda saw him and fixed both eyes on Max.

Lia did as he asked, belting out the words of the lullaby.

*"The Merryn's kiss, it gave her gills.
On softest weeds she lay."*

Skalda's pupils narrowed and again Max saw the tech behind its eyes glowing softly. "Do your worst, Skalda," he muttered, daring himself to stare right into the Beast's gaze. Straight away, he sensed electric currents burrowing through his brain, but this time nothing happened.

*"But a woman of land never will
A Merryn truly be. The day
Soon came when she longed for
Home, to breathe the air again."*

Max grinned. "It's working!" he cried. "Your singing stops the mind control."

Lia didn't look convinced. "How?"

"Does it matter?" said Max. "Probably

something to do with blocking the brain's signals. But don't you see?" he went on. "If it works on me, then perhaps we can break the barracuda's hold over the Sumarans."

He allowed himself a glance round at Lia and saw a flicker of hope in her eyes, but it quickly died. "What if you're wrong? The Merryn seem to be in a much deeper trance."

Skalda had stopped attacking, and waited patiently just beyond the entrance. *It knows its prey has nowhere to run*, thought Max.

"It must be because it's focusing its power on the other Merryn. That's why it can only control us for a short while." He pointed to the entrance to their cave. Skalda hovered, still as a statue. Max could almost feel the Beast's hunger. "Anyway, we don't have much choice that I can see. Either we wait in here to die, or we try to get away by singing."

Lia's jaw tightened and she nodded, joining

Max at the opening. "Okay. Let's split up to distract the Robobeast, then head back to the tunnels. Ready?"

Max allowed himself a grim smile and kicked out of the cave. Rivet and Spike shot out beside Lia. "Sing!" Max shouted.

They both broke into song as Skalda rounded on them, fixing him with his stare. Max wasn't exactly sure of the words, but the tune was easy enough. Lia climbed onto Spike and zipped towards the tunnels, while Max gripped Rivet's collar. "After her!" he yelled. By the time Skalda had figured out its mind control wasn't working, they were shooting through the gloomy tunnel.

Max turned and his heart lurched as he saw Skalda on their tail, squeezing its body into the tunnel. For a moment he dared to hope the Robobeast would be too big, but he saw Skalda edging after them, jaws snapping,

its metal plates rattling the sides of the passageway.

I just hope the Merryn soldiers aren't still waiting at the other end.

With Rivet's snout-lamp lighting a path ahead, Max led the way as fast as he dared. Max heard crashing behind him. The passageway widened closer to the exit and Skalda went even faster, smashing into the walls and scattering rocky debris in its wake.

"We need to buy some time!" said Lia.

Max drew his hyperblade, swam to the roof of the tunnel and jammed the blade into the rock. A crack opened up. Max pulled out the blade and stabbed again. With a low rumble, blocks of stone began to work loose.

"Hurry up!" screamed Lia.

Max saw Skalda's shadow approaching around a bend. He didn't have long. With a final lunge, he ran the hyperblade across the broken rock. The roof began to collapse and Max kicked himself clear. The rumble became a roar of falling stone, and when Max looked back, he saw a huge cloud of dust and debris in the water. As it cleared, he grinned. Boulders large and small were stacked up, almost completely blocking the tunnel.

"That should hold Skalda up for a while,"

he said. *But not forever.*

As soon as he'd spoken, Skalda hurled his body against the obstacle. The rocks quaked, but didn't budge. "Let's go!" said Max.

Spike shot through the gloom like a silver torpedo carrying Lia, and Max followed, gripping Rivet's collar.

They reached the Graveyard quickly, and paused at the entrance. "Stay here while I take a look," said Max. He peeked his head out from the opening. At first he thought it was all clear, until he noticed a couple of Merryn sitting on a discarded sub with their pearl lances across their laps. Beside them their swordfish steeds appeared to be dozing.

"Just two soldiers," said Max. "Ready to test my theory again?"

Lia nodded and they edged out of the tunnel, singing.

"*In olden times, there dwelt a maid...*"

The soldiers lifted their heads as one and leaped onto their swordfish.

"*Who longed...* It's not working! ...*the land,*" sang Lia.

"*To swim away...* Carry on!" Max replied.

The swordfish coursed towards them at

breakneck speed.

"*Of happiness in the sea,*" they chorused.

The soldiers levelled the points of their lances.

"*She dived beneath the waves one day…*" Max sang desperately, as the Merryn soldiers came at them.

He'd made a terrible mistake.

And now we're going to pay with our lives.

He closed his eyes and waited for death to come.

CHAPTER TWO

TRAITOR OF SUMARA

Lia's singing trailed off. Max tensed, ready for the stabbing pain of a pearl lance... but it never came.

Cautiously, he opened his eyes and saw both Merryn soldiers on their knees, bowing their heads.

"Princess," one said. "Please accept our humble apologies. I don't know what came over us."

"Arise," said Lia.

The other soldier looked bewildered. "What are we doing here?"

Spike was busy making friends with the other two swordfish, swimming in circles around them. Even Rivet was joining in the fun, his tail propeller wagging. Max saw that his aquabike was where he'd left it, stalled on its side not far from the opening.

"It's a long story," said Lia. "But here's the short version: there's a giant fish living beneath the city, and it's turned you all into slaves."

The soldiers looked at one another. "Princess, please don't jest with us," one said.

"She's telling the truth," Max said. "Take us back to the city and we'll show you."

"With pleasure," said the soldier.

Max climbed onto his aquabike while the three Merryn mounted their swordfish. It felt great to be back in the saddle.

"Fight bad man?" barked Rivet.

Max felt his knuckles tighten on the handlebars and he glanced across to Lia. She'd obviously heard Riv too, because she gave a determined nod. "That's right, boy," Max said. "It's time to make Regulis pay."

In no time at all, they were shooting under the Arch of Peace towards the palace. Again, the streets were deserted.

"Let us announce you," said one of the soldiers.

Lia shook her head. "I think that would be a bad idea," she replied. "Let's surprise Regulis."

"I'll go first," said Max. He pressed the throttle of the aquabike and boosted ahead of the others, aiming straight at the doors to the main chamber of the palace. He ducked low against the handlebars and braced himself for impact.

"Slow down!" cried one of the soldiers. "You're going to cra—"

The doors smashed inwards as the aquabike careered into them. Max looked back to see Lia, Spike and Rivet flooding in behind him. Regulis, seated on the throne, looked up. Around him, a dozen guards lowered their lances.

"Seize them!" cried Regulis.

The guards advanced as one, lowering their weapons, but Max was ready. He took a deep breath and began to sing.

"In olden times, there dwelt a maid..."

The lines of guards slowed, and a couple lowered their lances, but the rest kept coming. Then Lia joined in the singing. Even Rivet tried, but Max realised his dogbot needed new tuning software because the sound wasn't pretty. It sounded like he was chewing nails. The line of Merryn came to a halt completely and all the lances floated to the ground.

It worked! thought Max with a flood of relief. He peered past and saw Regulis already fleeing through a door at the rear of the chamber.

"Out of my way!" said Max, gunning the aquabike's engine.

The soldiers threw themselves to the ground as Max steered the aquabike over their heads in pursuit of Regulis. He entered a corridor lined with pillars, just wide enough for the bike to follow. The bike's wing caught a wall, sending a juddering shock through Max's arms, but he fought to keep it steady. Regulis swam ahead, throwing panicked glances over his shoulder.

You can run, but I'll catch you, thought Max.

The traitor Merryn veered left and down a set of steps. Max yanked the handlebars round hard, and the bike's rear end swung out and crunched into a wall.

Max could fix any dents later.

At the bottom of the stairs Regulis swam into a kitchen where Merryn cooks were preparing seaweed cakes on a long table.

They scattered as he shot past, and screamed when they saw the bike powering towards them.

"Sorry!" Max cried. When he'd almost caught Regulis, he slid a leg over the bike's saddle and then threw himself off. He landed on Regulis's back and they both rolled into a wall. The bike thumped into a

column, spun around and stalled.

Regulis was up first, and in a flash his coral sword was in his hand. Max drew his hyperblade.

"It's one on one, this time," said Max. "Give in, Regulis."

"Never!" said the Merryn. "No Breather tells me what to do."

He threw himself at Max, clawing with one hand and stabbing with his blade. Max backed away, and the blade's point nicked his wetsuit. Regulis lifted a leg and delivered a vicious kick to Max's midriff. He doubled up, gasping for breath. "Too easy!" snarled Regulis. He slashed down with his blade and Max rolled sideways just in time. Regulis's hyperblade lodged in the floor. As he tried to free it, Max whacked Regulis's sword arm with the flat side of his own hyperblade. Regulis dropped his weapon with a yelp.

Max pressed forward, breathing hard, and held his blade against the Merryn's throat.

"Not so easy, Regulis," he said. "Give in!"

The councillor held up his hands, a look of terror in his eyes. "Please," he said. "Don't kill me. I didn't want any of this. I didn't know what…"

"Enough!" Max interrupted. "Just tell me one thing: why aren't you affected by Skalda like everyone else?"

Regulis sighed, and Max backed away to give him some space. Even then, he kept his blade trained in case the Merryn tried anything.

But Regulis's shoulders sagged and he lowered his eyes. It was clear he was beaten.

"It started three days ago," he said. "A Breather woman visited Sumara. I was sent to meet her and she asked how I'd like to be king. I told her it was impossible, because

Sumara had a ruler, called Salinus. She just smiled strangely. She said that she could make me king in exchange for some of the crystals from the forest beneath the city – she wanted to pillage the entire crystal forest, and use the wealth to build more Robobeasts. She even provided the mining robots to get them."

Max remembered the strange spiked objects he'd seen in the cavern below Sumara. Could they have been these mining robots? *No doubt built by my uncle.*

"And did this visitor by any chance have an electric flail and one robotic leg?" asked Max.

Regulis's eyes lit up. "That's right! How did you know?"

Max shook his head in dismay. "Because Cora Blackheart is the most wicked pirate in all the seas of Nemos," said Max. "And you still haven't answered my question – why has everyone else turned into a brain-dead slave, when you're perfectly OK?"

Regulis smiled sheepishly. " Cora told me to make sure I was listening to music at dawn the following day. One of my jobs is to organise the palace entertainments, so it wasn't hard. I summoned some Grundle musicians, and asked them to audition for me. Reports started coming in that this giant fish was swimming down the central avenue. I thought everyone had gone mad, but sure enough, by the end of the day, the whole city was acting strangely. Even King Salinus seemed under some sort of spell. The one-legged Breather said I was in charge of the mining operation. She said the fish would stay underground, but that I could communicate with her at the Graveyard."

"The communication screen," said Max, as it all became clear. "And I bet you paid the Grundle with crystals, didn't you?"

"Yes," said Regulis, shame colouring his face.

A shadow approached, and Max turned to see Lia with a pearl lance, her face twisted with rage. "You rotten traitor!" she shouted.

Max threw himself between Regulis and Lia. "Wait!" he said.

"Out of my way!" Lia cried. "He doesn't deserve to live!"

Max shook his head. "You can't kill him,"

he said. "It's up to your father to decide what happens to Regulis."

Lia's lip was trembling with anger, and for a moment Max feared she might actually stab *him* to get to Regulis. But he stared hard into her eyes and after a moment passed, her expression softened and she lowered the lance. "Where's the *real* King?" she demanded.

Regulis swallowed. "I'll show you." he said.

Max narrowed his eyes. "Yes, you will. Right now."

CHAPTER THREE

SKALDA'S ARMY

"Salinus is in a cell in the prison," said Regulis.

"You locked him up!" said Lia. "You monster!"

Regulis held up his hands. "The pirate woman made me do it! She said that he resisted Skalda longer than the others, so the spell wasn't as strong."

"That's how he got a message to me," said Lia. "If you've done him any permanent damage, I'll make you pay."

Regulis led them down to the prison. It seemed empty at first, but when they came to the last cell Max saw King Salinus curled up at the back. He was wearing dirty robes, and his eyes seemed like empty hollows. Max remembered the old King Salinus, tall and slightly terrifying. This Merryn looked like a shadow of a King.

"Dad!" Lia cried.

Her father didn't move from the spot, but he lifted his eyes and stared vacantly at Lia.

"We need to sing," said Max, and started off the lullaby. Lia joined in too, tears pricking in her eyes. By the time the maiden in the song was getting tired of underwater life, King Salinus was shaking the curse from his head. He glanced quickly around, then straightened up, his face full of fury.

"What am I doing in here?" he bellowed. His eyes fell on Lia. "Daughter! Explain to me what's going on!"

"It's a long story," said Lia, unbolting the barred door. "But first, let's get you out of here."

Back in the palace's main chamber, Salinus sat on his throne, pearl spear clutched in his hand. Regulis cowered in front of him, ringed by twelve guards, all with their lances pointing at his chest.

"...and so Regulis took power," Max finished explaining. "Everyone else should be pardoned. No one – not even you, Your Majesty – is able to withstand Skalda's enchantment."

King Salinus had sat patiently while Max ran through Cora Blackheart's plot from the start. Max knew that it had taken a lot for the Merryn to trust him, a Breather, in the first place. Now he felt strangely guilty. Even though Cora's plan had nothing to do with him, she was a Breather too.

And in the back of his mind lurked Skalda. *This battle isn't over. We still have to deal with the Robobeast.*

Regulis whimpered. "Please, Your Majesty, if I may say a few words in my defence…"

"Silence!" boomed Salinus. "Take this wretch to the prison cells. Let's see how *he* enjoys it down there in the darkness."

Four of the guards seized Regulis and carried him away. The imposter king wailed in fear.

"And now, my rescuers," said the King, his tone softening as he turned to Max and Lia. "Sumara owes you a great debt."

Max blushed and smiled at Lia, when a guard ran through the main doorway, still hanging off its hinges where Max had driven the aquabike through.

"Your Majesty!" he cried, dropping to one knee. "The citizens – they're marching on the palace!"

Max, Lia and her father ran to the shattered doorway and gazed out. It was true. Hundreds of Merryn were advancing down the main avenue, under the Arch of Peace and coming towards the statue of Thallos. They swam in perfect time, slow but full of menace. Max's eyes travelled over the horde, then his heart stopped. At the very back, just a glinting shadow, swam Skalda.

It's turned the whole of Sumara against us.

The column grew closer by the second, and the Robobeast became clearer – tentacles bristling and ready to strike. Thankfully it was still too far away for its eyes to work their evil.

"How can we stop them?" said the King. "Even with all of us singing, there are too many of them for us to handle."

A sudden thought hit Max and he ran to the aquabike, taking out the Grundle music box. "It was Grundle music that protected Regulis," he said. "Let me try!"

He stood at the open doorway and held the music box aloft.

I hope this works.

He opened the box.

Nothing happened. Not a sound. Not a note. Nothing.

"What?" he said. "I don't understand."

"Never trust a Grundle," said King Salinus. He brandished his spear, but Max knew he would never use it against his own people.

We might not have a choice though, he thought. *It might come down to kill or be killed.*

"There must be some other way to stop them," said Lia.

As soon as she'd spoken, Rivet shot out of the door with Spike at his side. The dogbot swam right up to the forward line of Merryn, snapping his jaws. Spike darted in, swishing his sword in front of their faces. They didn't so much as blink.

"I know! We could barricade the doors," said Max, looking round for furniture to push up against them.

King Salinus shook his head. "There are other entrances. It would only hold them back for a short while."

Max's eyes went to his aquabike, parked beside the double doors, and a plan came suddenly to his mind. He swam over and pulled open the control panel. The bike had a loudspeaker for its underwater horn. It had been designed to warn oncoming subs to get out of the way, but Max had other ideas. He found the music player circuits and rewired them to the speakers.

"Max, this isn't the moment to be tinkering!" said Lia. "We need a plan!"

Max switched on the music player, and the palace walls practically shook with a booming mix of electronic sound. King Salinus and Lia both jumped and put their hands over their ears.

"What's the problem?" said Max, grinning. "The Psychotic Sharks are my favourite band!"

The other Merryn guards were cringing away as well.

No taste in music, thought Max.

Max climbed onto the bike, head banging to the thumping beat. He pushed the throttle and zoomed out through the gates, straight towards the advancing Merryn army.

He turned up the loudspeakers as high as they'd go, and the Psychotic Sharks' number-one hit – *Fishbait* – carried down the avenue. The front line of Merryn stalled and those behind them bumped into their backs. All at once, the massed ranks broke apart.

"It's working!" Max muttered to himself.

Soon all of the Merryn had stopped marching and stared at each other in confusion. The music came to an end with a

thrashing chord that echoed across the city. Max called out from the window.

"Citizens of Sumara!" he shouted. "You have been tricked by a powerful enemy. King Salinus is not your foe. Skalda the barracuda is the true threat to your city!"

The Merryn turned and saw the torpedo-like body of Skalda stalking in their wake. The Robobeast's green tech glowed.

Max raised his hyperblade and pointed it at his uncle's creation.

"It's time to defend Sumara!" he cried.

CHAPTER FOUR

THE TIDE TURNS

Rivet swam up alongside the aquabike.

"Get bad fish?" the dogbot barked.

"That's right," said Max. "Follow me, Riv."

He gripped the handlebars tightly and accelerated towards the Robobeast. The Merryn were gazing up at Skalda, obviously unsure what to do.

"Don't look into its eyes!" called Max, as he shot above the Merryn ranks. "Riv, I need you to activate your snout-cam and do some scouting of the robotics," he said. "I'll keep

Skalda busy while you're doing that."

"Yes, Max!" Rivet barked. With a burst of speed, he shot ahead. Skalda's tentacles writhed. As one swung down, Max leaned out of the bike's saddle and met it with his hyperblade, shearing a section away. A stream of bubbles rose from Skalda's flexing jaws. Another tentacle whipped around. Max nosed the bike beneath the Robobeast. Skalda twisted to follow him, and Rivet passed unseen above.

But then Max felt the Robobeast's hypnotic gaze settle on him. He tried not to look, but he couldn't help himself. The green eyes locked onto his and Max sensed the powerful tech burrowing into his brain, taking control...

His fingers found the music switch.

"*We're nothing but fishbait!*" screamed the Psychotic Sharks.

In a split second, Max's head cleared.

"You won't get me that easily!" he shouted over the twanging guitars.

He didn't see the tentacle until it was too late. It smashed into the side of the bike, almost throwing him from the seat. The music fizzed and died and Max realised the loudspeakers must have been damaged.

He righted himself on the bike and looked around. The green eyes found him again, and this time he couldn't look away. He felt

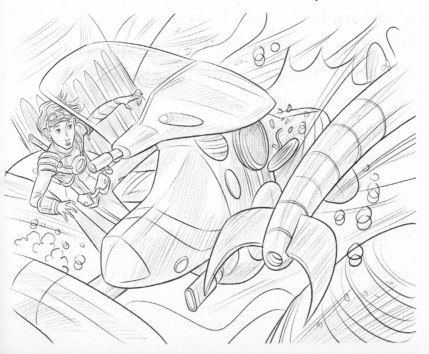

his brain grow heavy, and his thinking slow. A wave of anger swept into his heart.

Where's that pathetic robotic dog got to? he wondered. He saw it swooping over the barracuda, eyes on filming mode, analysing the robotics.

"Here, Riv!" Max called. He hid his hyperblade behind his back. When the dog came close enough, he'd give it a nasty surprise. *One stab with the hyperblade should be enough to scramble its circuits for good!*

Rivet came towards him, tongue lolling happily. "Rivet take pictures!" he barked.

Max's lip curled into a sneer, as he drew the hyperblade from behind him. "Maybe you can take a picture of this!" he said, lunging at the dogbot.

Rivet veered sideways, trying to dodge the blade, but it sliced into his tail propeller. "Max! No!" he barked, tail drooping between his legs.

"Rivet Max's friend!"

Max leaped off the bike and followed him. Rivet tried to swim away but his tail propeller dangled uselessly. "Time to go to the scrapyard," said Max, raising his hyperblade for the killing blow.

"Aargh!" he cried.

Fingers fastened onto his wounded arm, digging hard into the seaweed-covered gash. He saw they were webbed, and belonged to Lia. Hatred twisted her features as her other hand gripped his throat, closing his gills.

"I…can't…breathe," he said.

She squeezed harder. But Max still had his hyperblade. He drew it back, ready to thrust into her belly. *Wretched Merryn girl. This will teach you…*

Suddenly all the strength left his arm and the blade's tip stopped a finger's breadth from Lia's stomach.

Beautiful haunting music cascaded through the water in waves and drifting echoes. Lia's hands relaxed from his arm and throat, and Max's mind grew clear. *I've heard those sounds before. The Grundle!*

He looked around and saw the troop of Grundle musicians coming through the water, playing their strange instruments. He'd never been so glad to see the strange creatures.

"You took your time!" he said.

Rivet's alarm bark sounded, and Max

jerked a glance upwards. Skalda had the dogbot in a tentacle and tossed him from side to side in the water.

"Get off my dog!" Max roared, and jumped onto the aquabike. Rivet's eyes were flashing and Max imagined his circuits coming loose. He gunned the bike upwards, drawing his hyperblade.

CLANG!

He swung the blade at the robotic coil. It loosened a fraction, and Rivet scrambled to get free. Max swung at the tentacle again, then gripped the dogbot's back leg and yanked him out of danger.

To his relief, Max saw the rest of the Merryn were arriving, swarming through the water in formation, pearl lances bristling and ready. The Grundle led the way, playing their eerie music all the time.

"Keep the Robobeast busy!" Max shouted,

then sped the bike behind their lines. He needed to see what footage Rivet had managed to record. On the seabed, by the Arch of Peace, he jumped off the bike. Rivet's eyes were still flashing. "Lie still, Riv," he said, checking Rivet's tail. The circuits were mashed up from the fight with Skalda, but with the right tools he could get it fixed in no time.

"Max friend again?" asked Rivet, cowering away.

Max smiled and patted Rivet's head. "Sorry, boy. Max friend, yes. I wasn't myself for a moment there. Let's see what pictures you got for me."

He connected Rivet to the bike's monitor screen, then flicked through the footage at double speed. Rivet had done a full circuit of the Robobeast, zooming in on all the tech additions. But there was no sign of any control hub. Max began to lose hope.

But then he saw it.

A junction of wiring, at the roof of Skalda's mouth behind his teeth, glowed green under a metal mesh casing. Max paused the footage and zoomed in, but couldn't understand what he was looking at. The wires seemed to be sprouting from some sort of green gem – it didn't look like any tech he'd seen before. He pointed to the screen so Lia could see.

"I think that's some sort of computer

control box!" he said.

"Are you sure?" she asked.

"Positive," said Max, though part of him wished he was wrong. There was the small matter of those razor-sharp teeth to get past.

"Fall back!" cried a voice. It was King Salinus. "Everyone retreat!"

Max looked up, just as a Grundle harp fell to the ground, broken. He was stunned when, a moment later, a dead Grundle sank to the seabed as well.

The Merryn were turning and fleeing back towards the palace as Skalda attacked. Some of the Grundle bravely stood their ground, but their fear was making them play out of time. The barracuda's tentacles attacked without mercy.

They can only hold on so long. And without their music we're all doomed, thought Max.

King Salinus swam through the retreating

Merryn, desperation painted on his face.

"Skalda's too strong!" he cried. "Our weapons are useless."

Max looked at the chaos, fearing that the King was right.

CHAPTER FIVE

INTO THE JAWS

Even the Grundle had given up now, and the music went silent as they swam for their lives. Their leader passed near Max.

"I'm sorry, human, we tried our best."

Despair crept over Max's heart. *There has to be a way to defeat Skalda. If I can just distract him long enough to sneak into his mouth... But that's easier said than done.*

The Merryn were scattered, panicking. Max saw several looking up as Skalda swept above them. Then the Merryn began to fight one another. *The Robobeast is turning them again,* he realised. *One by one, they'll fall under his spell. And then they'll stop fighting each other, and fight us. We need to work as a team.* He called after King Salinus. "Your Majesty! Can you use your Aqua Powers to fight the Robobeast?"

The king frowned. "My powers aren't nearly enough."

"Not just you," Max said. "The whole city, concentrating as one."

A thin smile appeared on the King's lips. "That might work!" His voice boomed over the city. "Merryn, focus your powers on the barracuda. Give it everything you have!"

The people of Sumara who still had control of their minds paused. They turned to face the Robobeast with their eyes closed. Skalda glared at them, its green tech glowing brighter than ever.

Almost at once the Robobeast began to writhe like it was in pain, tentacles thrashing

and eyes rolling.

"This should settle the argument once and for all," said Lia. "Which is better, tech power or Aqua Powers!"

"For once, I don't care!" said Max. He'd happily lose their argument if it meant stopping his uncle's creature. He noticed Lia had closed her eyes too, pressing her hands to her temples to focus her powers. Skalda's green glow was fading, and the Merryn who were enslaved were shaking their heads as the Robobeast's trance lifted.

"Keep going!" bellowed King Salinus. "It's working!"

Hope blossomed in Max's chest. Skalda's tentacles began to droop, wafting gently in the water. *They're putting it under their own trance*, he realised. *Now for the hard part – getting into that mouth.*

"Don't stop!" said Max. He ditched the

aquabike. The less threatening he looked, the more likely Skalda would be to let him approach. Hopefully.

Rivet tried to follow. Max held up a hand. "Stay, Riv – you've done your part."

The dogbot cocked his head, then reluctantly sank down again.

Though Skalda lay practically still, his pupils wide, Max heart thumped faster and faster as he approached. *If I get this wrong, it's me who's fishbait*, thought Max.

By the time Max reached the Robobeast's slightly open mouth, the great fish was completely still in the water, tentacles limp.

He was about to swim into the gaping maw when he noticed movement on the seabed below and stopped. Something – no, *several* things – were burrowing up from below.

What now?

Small spiky objects burst from the ground,

and Max's heart sank. *The Professor's mining robots.* He paused, confused, half inside the deadly jaws.

Then it became clear. It was the bots causing the distant explosions and earthquakes. *The whirlpool too!* They were blasting bits out of the crystal columns holding up the seabed.

Before he could call out a warning, the mining bots shot towards the Merryn. Their

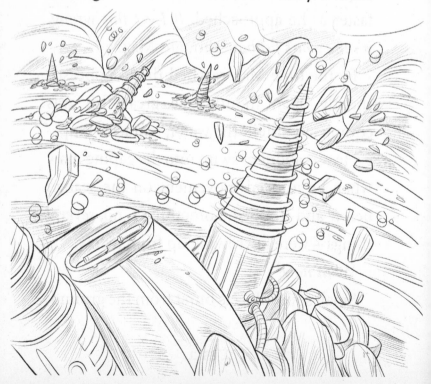

drill bits began to spin and whir. As the bots plunged into the massed ranks, the Merryn panicked, breaking their focus on Skalda.

Max felt a sudden current as Skalda's teeth descended towards his head.

He jerked forward, and darkness closed around him. He was trapped in the Robobeast's mouth. Almost at once, a powerful force snatched at his body.

Skalda's trying to swallow me!

Max flipped his body over and jammed his feet against the ridges lining the roof of the Beast's mouth, wrapping his arms around the nearest tooth. In the darkness, the control box gleamed dully. It wasn't far out of reach, attached to the roof of the Robobeast's mouth. But if he let go he'd be pulled down the black tunnel of the beast's throat. The glistening muscles clenched, opening and closing, creating suction. His arms strained against the force. He reached up and grabbed the next tooth, heaving himself towards the front of the mouth.

The jaws opened a crack and Max's heart dropped into his stomach. Through the narrow opening, he spied Lia and the other Merryn, all completely under the barracuda's sway once more. Several Grundle floated in the water too, their massive bodies limp and their instruments hanging loosely in their hands. He had to get through to them somehow, or he had no chance at all. He planted his feet on Skalda's lower jaw and pushed upwards with his hands, straining with the effort, until the jaws opened wider. He began to sing and his voice carried over the entranced crowd.

"In olden times there dwelt a maid..."

At first it didn't seem to have any effect, so Max belted out the words louder. Lia was the first to shake her head, her eyes finding their focus. Then her father broke free too. They both started to sing along.

"Keep singing!" said Max.

King Salinus's voice was rich and powerful, breaking the spell on several other Merryn. They sang as well, and soon the words of the lullaby sounded from all around.

We're winning! thought Max.

The barracuda shook from side to side, and Max had to lodge himself against a tooth to prevent Skalda hurling him out into the water. "You're not going to spit me out that easily!" he muttered.

The Merryn seemed to be overcoming the mining robots too, batting them away with their lances, or spearing them in mid-water.

"Rivet!" Max cried. "Keep Skalda busy!"

He saw his dogbot scoot up, slightly lopsided from his earlier encounter with the

Robobeast. Skalda went for him in a flash. Max threw himself back into the beast's mouth as its jaws snapped shut in front of him. Losing control, he slammed into each side of the throat as the barracuda thrashed, jerked and lurched through the water after Rivet. Max kept his eyes on the glowing green control box set behind the teeth. It was no larger than Rivet, and Max wedged his fingers under the covering panel and bent it over to get the workings beneath.

As he thought, all four cables linked directly into the green gem at the centre. What *was* that thing?

He took two cables in his hands and yanked them free. Skalda roared and thrashed, and Max slammed into the side of his mouth. He began to slip into the throat. *No!* He drew his hyperblade and jammed it into the control box, slowing his death-slide.

Muscles straining, he tugged himself back to the metal housing. "You're not getting rid of me that easily," he muttered. He grabbed the final two cables and tugged them loose as the throat strained to suck him down.

A sudden bang sounded, fading to a low hum. Skalda's body jerked and Max lost his grip. He tumbled into the depths of the throat, flailing helplessly against the current, searching for a grip on anything. All he felt was slippery flesh sliding beneath his fingers as he fell into the narrow gullet.

The phrase *eaten alive* came to him with a stab of terror.

Then the current shifted, throwing him the other way. He careered headlong back out into the mouth. Skalda's jaws were clamped shut and Max shot towards a wall of teeth, ready to break his neck or crush his skull.

He hoped it wouldn't hurt, at least.

CHAPTER SIX
A TEMPORARY PEACE

Light flooded over him, and Max found himself thrown into open water straight towards Lia. He saw her mouth, gaping with astonishment, a split second before he barrelled into her.

"Ouch!" she cried.

They rolled over together and came to a stop, surrounded by Grundle musicians.

Max twisted free and glanced at Skalda.

The Robobeast watched him with cold

yellow eyes. The green tint had vanished.

The Merryn had all fallen silent as they waited for Skalda's next attack. The barracuda flexed its jaws and gave a shudder, its flanks rippling with gold and black. Then with a clattering, grinding sound the face-plates fell away, the metal sinking to the seabed and

taking the limp tentacles with it.

"Hurray!" said Max, punching the water.

Spike edged close to the barracuda, twitching his sword. He didn't seem scared at all.

Skalda gave a couple of tail-flicks and turned a half-circle.

"It's saying thank you," said Lia, smiling.

Slowly at first, the barracuda began to swim away. Then, with a sudden thrust of speed, it was gone.

"Shall we play?" asked the leader of the Grundle.

Max shook his head, staring after the magnificent barracuda. "There's no need," he said. "I think we've all had enough music for today."

By the time the sun set over the ocean, the Grundle were long gone, drifting away on their strange journey into the depths. Sumara was a bustle of activity. Lines of Merryn were passing debris to the Graveyard, including the remains of the mining robots. Others were hard at work rebuilding the city's coral walls.

Max and Lia were in the throne chamber, making repairs to Rivet, while a team of Merryn were rehanging the battered doors. Lia had applied a new seaweed bandage to the wound on Max's arm. The gash was healing quickly in the salt water, much quicker than on land.

"So I think this proves once and for all," she said, "Aqua Powers won the day."

Max, running checks on Rivet's sensors, grinned. "Er...but wasn't I the one who dismantled the control box in Skalda's throat?"

King Salinus swam up to them. "Are you

two arguing again?" he said, with a grin. "Maybe it's time to call a truce and accept it was a combination of tech and Aqua Powers that allowed us to triumph? It took both of you to save our city."

Max shared a glance with Lia. "Hmmm… maybe," he said.

Lia looked more seriously at the King. "Father, what will happen to Regulis?"

King Salinus's face darkened. "He will be tried and punished accordingly. Exile would be the best punishment, I think."

"Wouldn't it be safer to keep him locked up?" asked Lia. "If he's free to roam the seas, what will stop him teaming up with Cora again?"

King Salinus placed a comforting hand on his daughter's shoulder. "Don't worry – we've destroyed the communication screen at the Graveyard. The Breather woman has no way to contact Regulis."

"Besides," Max added, "I doubt Cora looks too kindly on those who fail her."

With his arm bandaged again, Max set to work fixing Rivet's tail propeller with a soldering torch. When it was spinning normally again, Rivet swam in happy circles.

But Max found himself casting an anxious glance upwards.

"I don't need my Aqua Powers to know what you're thinking," said Lia. "You want to go home, don't you?"

Max nodded. He'd only had a few hours of being reunited with his mother and father. There was so much to talk about, and he barely knew where to begin.

"You should go," Lia said. "We can finish the repairs here without you."

"Thank you," said Max, "but are you sure?" It felt odd to leave Sumara, and Lia. He realised he'd miss them both.

"Your parents will be worried about you," said Lia.

Max closed Rivet's hatch. "Come on, Riv. We'll give you a proper tune-up on land!"

He swam to the palace doors, to find his aquabike. On the threshold, he looked back at Lia.

"I don't think it will be long before I'm in the sea again."

"Because you'll miss the seaweed cakes so much?" said Lia, grinning.

"Something like that," Max replied. "I'll see you soon."

As he jumped onto the saddle and checked the control panel, Max's mind lingered on Lia's joke. It took him a minute to realise what bothered him about it.

It won't be seaweed cakes that bring me back beneath the waves.

It will be Cora Blackheart.

Her revenge might not come quickly, but it would come for certain. And when it did, Max had no doubt it would be terrible. He thought about the mining robots, the remains of which had been gathered up and taken to the Graveyard. Max couldn't help wondering just how much of the precious crystal the robots had gathered for Cora. With the wealth she must have accumulated, there was no telling what she might be able to do next.

Rivet was already swimming upwards, homing in on Aquora.

Max took a deep breath and gunned the aquabike towards home. He was climbing high above the towers of Sumara beside the robodog when a voice called from behind. "Wait for me!"

Lia was rising from the palace on Spike, a

wide grin on her face.

"I had second thoughts," she said. "I'll join you on land, Breather. You need someone to look after you. Just in case."

"Is that right?" said Max.

A blush rose to Lia's cheeks. "Like my dad

said, we make a good team. Don't we?"

"Good team!" barked Rivet.

"Not just a *good* team," said Max. "The best!"

And together, they sped through the seas towards Aquora and the adventures that lay ahead of them.

Don't miss the next Sea Quest book,

in which Max faces

REKKAR
THE SCREECHING ORCA

Read on for a sneak preview!

CHAPTER ONE

THE LEAPING DOLPHIN RETURNS

Max crouched on a platform, welding torch in hand, working on the body of the *Leaping Dolphin II*. The submarine was held in place above the water by four huge clamps. As Max directed the blue flame over the join between two metal plates, sparks showered off the hull and sizzled when they hit the water. Meanwhile his dogbot Rivet dashed back and forth, trying to catch the sparks in his mouth.

Beyond the docks, the tall skyscrapers of the city rose like needles into the clouds. Transports hovered through the streets, and cranes lifted huge steel beams into place. Since Cora Blackheart's attack just weeks earlier, the repairs had gone on day and night. Her Robobeast Chakrol had destroyed a huge section of the city's titanium defence shield and left much of the fleet badly damaged.

The waves beside the dock stirred and Max's friend Lia's head emerged. Her Amphibio mask dangled from her neck by a strap, and she placed it over her nose and mouth to allow her to breathe above the water. The Merryn princess pushed silver hair away from her face with a webbed hand.

"Still tinkering with that lump of metal?" she said.

"Rivet not lump!" said Max's robodog.

Max killed the blowtorch and raised his protective visor. "Not any more. I'm done!" he said, feeling a swell of pride in his chest. He patted Rivet's snout. "She's not talking about you, boy." He stood up and admired his handiwork – a full-size replica of the first *Leaping Dolphin*, gleaming in the early morning light – *Leaping Dolphin II*.

Not just any lump of metal, thought Max. The submarine's sleek body was shaped like a bullet, with a plexiglass viewing screen at the front and portholes along the side. Four thrusters were positioned at the front and rear, their steel propellers polished to a shine. There was a hatch on top and an airlock for leaving or entering underwater. Emblazoned across the vessel's flank in scarlet paint was a stencil of an arcing dolphin.

Max's mother, Niobe, stuck her head through the hatch. "I'm finished in here too," she said, climbing out and jumping down from the top of the sub. "Hi, Lia!" She stood back and squeezed Max's shoulder. "It looks even better than the original, Max. Thank you!"

Max grinned. The first *Leaping Dolphin*

was now a shipwreck, lost beneath the waves. So for the last fortnight, he and his mother had been sourcing parts to build the replacement submarine. Finally, it was ready.

"Shall we take it for a spin?" asked his mother with a wink.

"Now?" said Max, glancing up at the towering skyscraper beside them. Their apartment was on the 523rd floor. "What about Dad?"

"Callum needs his sleep," said his mother. "He's working long shifts on the city's repairs. We'll be back before he's finished breakfast."

"All right then," said Max, excitement bubbling in his stomach. He missed the seas of Nemos. Especially since his aquabike had gone missing from the docks a couple of weeks ago. Someone must have stolen it, and so far the Aquoran cops hadn't managed to track the thief. *They've got plenty of other things to worry about, what with the damaged city*, Max thought glumly.

"I don't get it," said Lia. "It's still just a lump of metal, if you ask me."

The Merryn girl tried to look unimpressed, but Max could tell from the gleam in her eyes she was faking.

"Come on," he said. "Let's take a look inside."

They climbed aboard, dropping through the top hatch. Rivet scrambled through last, dangling for a moment by his front claws before landing with a clang. Much of the interior looked the same as Max remembered – the twin seats at the front covered with red leather, the storage facilities and scanning equipment. But looking closer, Max realised his mother had equipped the new *Leaping Dolphin* with several upgrades. "Awesome!" he said, running his fingers over the controls.

The sensors had a longer reach. He switched on the navigation systems and saw they were Compass 3.0, the most advanced available. "How did you get your hands on this?" he asked.

His mum's eyes shone with excitement. "I pulled a few strings. Check this out." She pushed a button and two gauntlets rose out of the control panel. "Manual grapplers," she said. "Put your hands in."

Max did as she said, and slid his hands into the gloves. As he did so, two metal claws extended from beneath the sub's nose. They clenched and opened as Max flexed his fingers.

"Cool!" he said. "And what about these?"

He pointed to a bank of switches and a control stick. His mother grabbed his hand and pulled it back. "Those are the new weapons systems," she said gravely. "I've fitted blasters and torpedoes."

Max nodded, feeling suddenly serious. The original *Dolphin* had been an exploratory vessel, but this one could defend itself.

I just hope it doesn't have to.

COLLECT THEM ALL!

SERIES 1:

978 1 40831 848 5   978 1 40831 849 2   978 1 40831 850 8   978 1 40831 851 5

SERIES 2: THE CAVERN OF GHOSTS

978 1 40832 411 0   978 1 40832 412 7   978 1 40832 413 4   978 1 40832 414 1

SERIES 3: THE PRIDE OF BLACKHEART

978 1 40832 853 8   978 1 40832 855 2   978 1 40832 857 6   978 1 40832 859 0

www.seaquestbooks.co.uk

COMING SOON: SERIES 4
THE LOST LAGOON

DON'T MISS THE NEXT SPECIAL BUMPER EDITION, DRAKKOS THE OCEAN KING, IN NOVEMBER 2014

WIN AN EXCLUSIVE GOODY BAG

In every Sea Quest book the Sea Quest logo is hidden in one of the pictures. Find the logo in this book, make a note of which page it appears on and go online to enter the competition at

www.seaquestbooks.co.uk

Each month we will put all of the correct entries into a draw and select one winner to receive a special Sea Quest goody bag.

You can also send your entry on a postcard to:

Sea Quest Competition, Orchard Books, 338 Euston Road, London, NW1 3BH

Don't forget to include your name and address!

GOOD LUCK

Closing Date: 30th September 2014

Competition open to UK and Republic of Ireland residents. No purchase required. For full terms and conditions please see www.seaquestbooks.co.uk

DARE YOU DIVE IN?

www.seaquestbooks.co.uk

Deep in the water lurks a new breed of Beast.

Dive into the new Sea Quest website to play games,
download activities and wallpapers and read all
about Robobeasts, Max, Lia, the Professor
and much, much more.

Sign up to the newsletter at www.seaquestbooks.co.uk
to receive exclusive extra content, members-only
competitions and the most up-to-date
information about Sea Quest.

IF YOU LIKE SEA QUEST, YOU'LL LOVE BEAST QUEST!

FREE COLLECTOR CARDS INSIDE!

Series 1: COLLECT THEM ALL!

An evil wizard has enchanted the magical beasts of Avantia. Only a true hero can free the beasts and save the land. Is Tom the hero Avantia has been waiting for?

978 1 84616 483 5

978 1 84616 482 8

978 1 84616 484 2

978 1 84616 486 6

978 1 84616 485 9

978 1 84616 487 3

DON'T MISS THE BRAND NEW SERIES OF:

FREE COLLECTOR CARDS INSIDE!

Series 14: THE CURSED DRAGON

RAFFKOR
THE STAMPEDING BRUTE

978 1 40832 920 7

VISLAK
THE SLITHERING SERPENT

978 1 40832 921 4

TIKRON
THE JUNGLE MASTER

978 1 40832 922 1

FALRA
THE SNOW PHOENIX

978 1 40832 923 8

OUT NOW!